★ TODAY'S ★
HEROES

David Robinson

Other books in the Today's Heroes Series

Joni Eareckson Tada
Colin Powell
Ben Carson

★ TODAY'S ★ HEROES

David Robinson

Gregg & Deborah Shaw Lewis

Zonder**kidz**

Today's Heroes: David Robinson
Copyright © 2002 by Gregg and Deborah Shaw Lewis

Requests for information should be addressed to:

Zonderkidz™
The children's group of Zondervan

Grand Rapids, Michigan 49530
www.zonderkidz.com

ISBN: 0-310-70297-6

Photography © AFP/CORBIS
Cover Design: Lookout Design Group
Interior design by Todd Sprague
Printed in the United States of America

02 03 04 05 06 07 / DC/ 10 9 8 7 6 5 4 3 2 1

CONTENTS

MORE THAN A CELEBRITY

The first time David Robinson walked into their classroom, all the fifth graders at Gates Elementary School in San Antonio, Texas, looked up. Way up!

Of course, they had known he was tall. You can't play center for the San Antonio Spurs and be an NBA all-star without being a very big man. But watching professional basketball players running back and forth on a TV screen, even if it's a large screen, doesn't really prepare you to have a seven-foot, one-inch giant standing over your desk at school.

The year was 1991. And one of the greatest basketball players in the world was paying a visit to a school in one of the poorest neighborhoods on San Antonio's Eastside. Why? His mother asked him to.

Although the neighborhood was just a few blocks from one of the city's most popular tourist attractions, the ritzy, glitzy River Walk, the dilapidated buildings of the Eastside had a profound impact on the athlete. It seemed to be a place where dreams too often die. "A lot of kids were getting into drugs and crime," David Robinson said. "You grow up in that circle and that's all you see." He couldn't get over the fact that many kids never got past the ten- to fifteen-block area where they grew up.

Freda Robinson, David's mother, attended and taught Sunday school at an Eastside church. She knew some of the teachers, and she'd met many of the African-American and Hispanic students enrolled at Gates Elementary. She believed the kids she'd met needed someone to look up to in more ways than one—someone like her son David.

Mrs. Robinson believed that the fifth graders she'd met had a lot of potential. But because they came from poor families—many from unhappy or tragic backgrounds—the odds were stacked against them. She knew that most of the kids at Gates Elementary would eventually drop out of school. Perhaps she could find a way to encourage and inspire them to strive for their potential. That's when she decided to propose a radical idea to her son.

"Mom always had a heart for the community and for those kids," David says. "So she came to me and said, 'I've got a great idea that could really make a difference in kids' lives.' I'd always believed in the value of education, and after I met the kids I thought, *This really could work! Now's the time to get kids started thinking about their futures. If in fifth grade kids believe it really is possible they could go to college someday, they will begin planning and aiming for that goal. We just need to help them realize the opportunity will be there.*"

So what was this idea designed to inspire kids from San Antonio's Eastside? David told all ninety fifth graders at Gates Elementary that if they stayed in school and graduated from high school, he would give each graduate $2,000 to use for college or technical school training.

Those fifth graders could hardly believe it. Two thousand dollars apiece! David had to smile at their excitement. But he also told them in a rather stern tone, "You better take it seriously and say to yourself, 'Man I want to make something out of myself.'" He told them that he was willing to set aside more than enough money to buy himself a nice Porsche. So he expected them to work hard.

David Robinson's scholarship promise was only part of the plan. Mrs. Robinson set up monthly progress meetings at the school to check up on the kids and talk to their teachers. David became a regular visitor at Gates Elementary, giving pep talks and advice to the students and getting to know the kids.

As the years passed and those students moved on to middle school and then high school, David and his mother stayed in touch with them. In addition to the regular monthly progress meetings, there were big annual get-togethers for the kids and sometimes their families—cookouts at David's parents' house and outings at a major amusement park.

In 1998 about fifty of those kids from Gates Elementary received their high school diplomas. David attended the graduation ceremony for twenty-five of them at Sam Houston High in San Antonio. "People say I've given them this, but really these kids have given me a lot more," David said. "I went to that graduation, and I felt like a dad to twenty-five kids. How cool is that?"

There is no way of knowing how many of those kids would have stayed in school if David Robinson hadn't made them that promise back in 1991. But if you talk to them one at a time today, student after student will tell you that the San Antonio Spurs' MVP center has also been a "most valuable player" in their lives.

Homer Adams III, now a student at Tuskegee University, said he had never been anywhere near a basketball star until David Robinson visited his fifth-grade classroom. Now he calls him Dave and sees his personal friend's determination on the basketball court as an example he can match with his own commitment to succeed.

Chris Mackey played basketball for four years at Sam Houston High School. When he didn't win an athletic scholarship, David Robinson challenged him to consider going on to college anyway. "He wasn't just a celebrity on TV. He was there in person," Mackey says. "He's not a person who just went to the NBA. He finished school first." Chris is trying to follow that example. He's now a Prairie View A & M student who says, "I'm just blessed to be in college."

"The majority of us who were in that group of fifth graders at Gates Elementary are in college," says Roderick Thomas who is now studying architecture. "I just feel that the number would be smaller if he hadn't adopted our class."

But adopting an entire class of students and promising to help them pay for college isn't the only reason David Robinson qualifies as one of today's heroes. His life on and off the basketball court has inspired so many people over the years that *Sports Illustrated* once ran a feature story about him with a close-up cover photo titled "Saint David."

He's quick to say he's not a saint. Yet David Robinson does have an impressive story—one that neither begins nor ends with his involvement in the lives of fifth graders from Gates Elementary School.

2

A TERRIBLE ACCIDENT

One morning in February, 1966, Freda Robinson drove her husband Ambrose to work. An expert in sonar—a type of radar that scans things underwater—Mr. Robinson was headed for South Africa aboard the U.S.S. Van Voorhis.

In the car with them were their children, two-year-old Kim and six-month-old David. Mrs. Robinson knew her husband would be gone for some time, so she had decided that she and the children would visit her sister in Rye Beach, New Hampshire, for the next several days.

The Robinsons lived in Newport, Rhode Island, only a two-hour drive from Rye Beach. Ordinarily such a short trip would be no problem. But on this particular day, an ice storm had been predicted.

Concerned about the approaching bad weather, Mr. Robinson urged his wife not to make the trip to New Hampshire. But once she had dropped her husband off at the ship, she searched the sky and decided the weather didn't look that bad. So she packed some clothes for herself and the kids and left for New Hampshire anyway.

The drive turned out to be uneventful, and the Robinson family had a good time visiting with Freda's sister Jessie, her husband Mitch, and their six children. But two days after they arrived, the ice storm finally arrived. The storm was so bad that only emergency vehicles were allowed on the road.

Mrs. Robinson got up that morning, took David out of his crib, and laid him on her bed. She left him there while she went into the kitchen to heat his bottle. While she waited for the bottle to get warm, she talked to her sister Jessie.

David's mother noticed that he had stopped crying, but she assumed he had fallen back asleep and kept visiting with Jessie.

When David's mother walked back into the room and did not see David on the bed, she quickly searched the floor, believing that he must have fallen off the bed. But she was not able to find him.

Mrs. Robinson's mind was swimming. Maybe her brother-in-law Mitch had picked up the baby. Running to the door of his room, she called out.

"Mitch, do you have David?"

"No," he answered.

"Don't kid me," David's mother told him.

Mitch came out in his bathrobe and repeated, "I don't have him, Freda."

Now Mrs. Robinson was near panic. "Well, where is he?" She ran into the living room and asked the other children. "Is David here?"

"No, ma'am," they answered.

She ran back into the bedroom and looked again: beside the bed, under the bed, on the bed. Suddenly she saw the top of his head. He had fallen between the bed and the wall and was jammed between the two. He was hanging there, his face tightly pressed into the mattress.

Grabbing him up, Mrs. Robinson noted that he had turned blue. As a nurse she knew that babies turn blue when they don't get enough oxygen. She was standing there crying loudly and pacing when her sister Jessie ran into the room.

"Stop it!" Jessie told her sister. "He will be dead if you don't give him CPR."

"I can't," David's mother sobbed. "I've never done CPR on a human. I've only done it on a mannequin."

"If you don't want him to die, you had better try," Jessie urged her.

Mrs. Robinson laid baby David down on the mattress and started the CPR that she had been trained to do, and she began to pray—loudly. Freda had always believed that God answers prayers. So she cried, "Lord, please don't let my baby die!"

Mrs. Robinson put her fingers into David's mouth, sweeping to see if he had anything blocking his airway. He didn't. She put her ear against his chest and listened but could not hear him breathing. So she leaned over, tipped his head back, and breathed into his mouth and nose. She paused for three seconds and then blew air into his mouth again. David still wasn't breathing.

She blew another small breath into David's lungs, then paused three seconds and blew again.

She saw his little chest rise.

Jessie was watching too. "It looks like he's breathing," she exclaimed.

Mrs. Robinson picked David up and saw his eyes roll back in his head. She thought he was about to go into convulsions. So she ran out of the bedroom, through the kitchen and into the garage. She knew the cold air in the garage would shock him. And it worked! David's eyes stopped rolling, and he began to cry.

Mitch called for an ambulance, but with the roads in such bad shape from the weather, it took the emergency crew longer than usual to get to the house. While they waited, David's mother wrapped him in blankets and tried to warm him up.

Finally, the emergency crew arrived. When they saw David, he was no longer blue. In fact, he looked just fine to them. He was just cold.

They took him to the hospital where he was put in an isolette to help get his temperature back to normal. Still Mrs. Robinson worried. She was, after all, a nurse, so she knew a person can go without oxygen only four to six minutes. After that, brain damage occurs.

When the doctors asked Mrs. Robinson how long David had been blue, she couldn't tell them. She wasn't sure how long she had been in the kitchen talking and laughing with her sister Jessie. And she had no idea how long it had taken David to scoot across the mattress, fall down between the mattress and the wall, and get jammed so tight that he couldn't breath.

She must have been out of the room at least five minutes, maybe several minutes longer. She hoped David had not been in distress that long. But there was no way to know for sure, so there was no way for the doctors to tell if—or how much—brain damage might have occurred.

"I'll have to wait until he starts learning and talking?" David's mother asked the doctor.

"That's about the size of it," he responded.

Now Mrs. Robinson had two things to worry about. How would they cope if David had indeed suffered brain damage and how would she tell her husband, especially since he had asked her not to go to New Hampshire in the first place.

Since her husband was at sea, Mrs. Robinson couldn't telephone him. She had to let him know what had happened in a letter.

Two days later, Jessie asked Freda to drive her to a local shopping center. The roads were still icy but she agreed. In the 1960s, cars were not equipped with seat belts and baby car seats had not yet been invented. His mother laid David down on the seat beside her in the car.

On the way to the shopping center, another driver lost control of her car on the ice and slid into their car, hitting on David's side of the vehicle. David was not hurt. But Freda then had to write her husband another letter, describing yet another near tragedy that would not have happened if she had stayed home as he had asked her to. Ambrose was particular about the car, and she hated to have to tell him it had been so badly damaged.

Finally, her husband got the letters and was able to call home. "Are you all right?" he asked. "Is David hurt? Did Jessie get hurt?"

Freda explained that the only casualty was the car. Ambrose was relieved to hear that his family was safe. He did not scold her for going to her sister's house. Mrs. Robinson was happy that her husband was more concerned about his family than the car. She felt bad enough as it was.

Her husband's reaction was one less thing to worry about, but Mrs. Robinson still had to face a more daunting concern. How long had David been without oxygen? Had he suffered brain damage while he hung trapped between the wall and the mattress that icy morning?

Three years is a long time to worry about something that important. But that is how long the Robinsons had to wait for their answers.

3

EARLY READER

Freda Hayes had met Ambrose Robinson at church one Sunday. He was in the Navy, stationed in Rhode Island. Freda was in nursing school in New Hampshire. She wanted to finish school and wasn't interested in getting serious about a boyfriend.

Since Ambrose was engaged to another woman, Freda thought that it was safe to be friendly with him. After church that Sunday they talked for a while and then Freda invited him to come to the house and meet her family.

Ambrose's naval duties kept him at sea for months at a time. But whenever he came home, he would visit New Hampshire to see Freda.

On one of his leaves, Ambrose showed up at the nursing home where Freda was working part-time and asked if she could leave work and go out with him. It was a curious request and Freda assured Ambrose that she could not leave. She had just begun her shift and would be on duty until 11:00 that evening. But Ambrose persisted, asking her to find someone else to work her shift.

Freda finally agreed to call two of her fellow nurses' aides. The first was a woman with small children who could not come in on short notice. The second was a friend named Helen. Freda often filled in for Helen so that she could do things with her husband. Yet Helen did not want to come into work that night.

"Let's call your boss and talk with her," Ambrose persisted.

Freda's supervisor, Mrs. Callahan, lived in the top floor of the nursing home, but Freda did not want to ask her boss for the evening off. Still Ambrose kept insisting.

So Freda called and Mrs. Callahan came downstairs. Freda introduced her to Ambrose who told Mrs. Callahan that he had been at sea for three months and desperately wanted to spend the evening with Freda.

"What is she to you?" Mrs. Callahan asked.

"She is my fiance," he answered.

That was news to Freda!

Mrs. Callahan gave the go-ahead.

As Freda and Ambrose walked across a playground, heading from the nursing home to her house, Freda scolded him, "Why did you tell that woman a lie? We aren't engaged! You are going to get me fired. And I need this job!"

"I didn't lie," he answered. "We *are* going to get married."

And less than three weeks later, Freda Hayes and Ambrose Robinson did get married. The following year, their daughter Kimberly was born. Two years after that, on August 6, 1965, Freda had their second child, David Maurice Robinson.

★

In 1966, several months after Mrs. Robinson's near-disastrous visit to her sister's house that wintry February weekend, the Navy transferred her husband to Key West, Florida. The family lived there until David was three years old. One day while the Robinsons were traveling on a highway near Key West, their questions about whether or not David had suffered brain damage were answered.

The speed limit was 55 miles per hour, but Mr. Robinson was driving about 60 miles per hour. Three-year-old David stood up in the back seat, looked over his father's shoulder, and announced, "Daddy, you're speeding!"

"Oh really?" his father protested.

David pointed to a speed limit sign along the side of the road and then to the dashboard.

"The speed limit is 55," David said. "And you're going 60."

David's parents looked at each other. They were surprised and relieved! If their three-year-old son could read the road sign and understand the measurement on a speedometer, it was almost certain his brain was functioning just fine.

Actually, the Robinsons had suspected the truth for some time. Every morning, Mrs. Robinson would call Kimberley and David in to watch *The Dr. Seuss Show*, a television program they enjoyed. They would pull up their chairs in front of the TV and when the host of the show announced which Dr. Seuss book they would be reading that day, David and Kimberley would grab the right book and read along.

David had not yet begun school, so the Robinsons didn't know if he was reading the books or if he had memorized them. But David surely was showing a healthy interest in books and reading.

Mrs. Robinson liked reading to her children and had story time with them almost every night. She made a game of learning and reading. Their family had a chalkboard on which Mrs. Robinson and the children could write words, and a bulletin board where they put up little notes. She had a yardstick, which the children used for measuring. Even when their family traveled, they read road signs, license plates, and the names of the cars they passed as they drove down the road.

The Florida weather was usually warm and nice in Key West. One of David's favorite activities was riding his toy tractor. Sitting on the black seat of that green tractor, David would pedal up and down the sidewalks around their apartment complex.

It was a pleasant place to live, but things were not easy for the Robinsons. David's mother worked long hours at the hospital, and his father was often at sea for as many as 250 days out of the year, leaving Mrs. Robinson to raise two small children by herself. When he was at home, Mr. Robinson often invited his Navy buddies to the house where they competed to see who could drink the most beer. Mrs. Robinson decided that she wanted a divorce.

She talked to Liz, a friend at work, who was a divorced nurse's aide.

"Divorce is no picnic!" Liz told her friend. "Your husband is a good provider. He loves you and your kids! Why do you want to get rid of him?"

"I'm tired," Freda told her. "I can't handle this anymore."

Liz tried to talk Freda out of the divorce. But when Freda insisted, Liz recommended a lawyer.

Freda called her parents and asked for money to help pay for the lawyer. But her parents liked Ambrose and didn't think Freda had enough reason to divorce him. So they refused to send her money to help her leave her husband.

Still, Freda called the attorney's office to make an appointment. But the lawyer couldn't see her for two weeks.

"I have to see him very soon!" Freda protested.

"Is it a matter of life and death?" the receptionist asked.

"Yes!" Freda answered, so the lawyer agreed to see her during his lunch break that same day.

He listened to her problems and then told her, "You and your husband just need to learn how to communicate."

So the lawyer wrote Ambrose a letter. The next Saturday, David's parents went to see the lawyer together. They took Kimberly and David with them.

When the lawyer saw Kimberly and David in the outer office, he exclaimed, "What precious children!" And he had his secretary give them cookies while he talked to Mr. and Mrs. Robinson in the inner office.

"Do you want to save this marriage?" he asked Ambrose.

"By all means!" Ambrose answered.

"Do you want to save this marriage?" he asked Freda.

"I guess so," Freda told him.

The lawyer spent forty-five minutes talking to them about how to work through their problems. By the time they left that day, both Freda and Ambrose were determined to make their marriage work.

4

THE HUMAN CALCULATOR

When David Robinson was four years old, his family moved to Norfolk, Virginia. The state of Virginia, at that time, did not offer public kindergarten. Feeling that all children need to attend kindergarten, David's parents scrimped and saved the money to send him to a private kindergarten at a Lutheran church.

By the time he began first grade, his family lived in military housing on the Naval Base in Norfolk. It didn't take the teachers at his school long to discover that David Robinson was a very bright little boy.

One day at the beginning of the school year, David's teacher gave the students a test. David did so well that the teacher thought there might have been a mistake. She gave David another test similar to the first and again he did remarkably well. Amazed, the teacher spoke with the principal who placed David in a room near his office, away from the other children, and tested him one more time. David did even better on the last test than he had on the others.

Soon David's intelligence began to create problems in the classroom. He would finish his work faster than any of the other children and get everything right. But once he was finished, he would distract the other children who were still working.

The principal and teachers called Mr. and Mrs. Robinson in for a conference. Maybe David needed to be in second grade, instead of first, they suggested. He was doing so well that the other students were beginning to feel as if they were behind.

His parents didn't want David to skip to second grade. They felt it was important for him to be treated like a normal kid, so they asked David's teachers to let him do some second-grade, maybe even third-grade, work when he finished his first-grade activities. That would keep him busy and learning. Then he wouldn't have time to bother the other children. The plan worked well. David thrived on the advanced work, and he no longer had time to bother the other children.

When David's dad came home from work, he would often sit down and play his favorite pieces on the piano. He had studied piano for ten years while he was growing up and played the piano in church as a teenager. Freda had admired the way Ambrose would play the piano for her when they were dating. Ambrose found it relaxing after a long day at work, and David loved to climb on his father's lap while he played.

One evening when David was five years old, Mr. Robinson had been playing piano with David next to him. Ambrose got up for a minute and walked into another room. A few moments later he was surprised to hear a familiar tune. David's parents walked in to see David at the piano playing the same song his father had just been playing.

"David!" his father exclaimed. "How did you learn to play that song?"

"I just watched you play, Dad," David explained.

David's dad immediately recognized that the boy was unusually talented and decided he should begin to teach David about music. He got the sheet music that he had used while taking piano lessons as a boy and used it to teach David, who turned out to be a quick learner. David soon learned to read and play from written music and compose songs of his own. One of the first songs David played was "Moonlight Sonata," a difficult classical piece.

Just one month before David's sixth birthday, his younger brother Chuck was born. When his parents brought Chuck home from the hospital, David seemed to think he was a neat new toy.

By the time David started second grade, he was chosen to participate in a new program for gifted children. One day a week he and other gifted children from all over town went to a magnet school to take classes that would challenge them. The classes were held in two trailers behind the school.

David liked the gifted program. Being around other really bright kids gave him a chance to work at being the best in a group of others who were the best. At last, he felt challenged.

When David was in third grade, he loved to go shopping with his mother. After making out a grocery list, she and David would walk across a little bridge to the store together.

David's mother called him her "human calculator." By the time they reached the checkout line, David had already totaled in his head the prices of the grocery items they had chosen. He could tell his mother exactly how much their groceries would cost. If it was going to cost more money than his mother had to spend, David could tell her what she needed to put back on the shelf. And David also helped her figure out which items were the best buy.

★

Every day Kim and David came home from school tired and hungry. So their mom would let them eat a snack and rest a little before starting their homework. But Mrs. Robinson refused to let them go anywhere or do anything else until their homework was completed.

David often finished all his homework while he was at school. But his parents thought he needed to study anyway. His mother often gave him extra books to read or some higher level work to do every afternoon.

When Kim and David had questions about their homework, their mom made them look up the answers. She knew they were more likely to remember those things that they looked up for themselves.

Sometimes when Kim or David didn't have anything to do, their dad would give them a page out of the dictionary and say, "Learn as many of these words as you can." Then he would come back later and quiz them. He thought of himself as one of their teachers. He loved to watch them learn.

David and Kim liked to learn new words to use in the many games, like Scrabble, they played together as a family

David loved to read. One Saturday when he was in the fifth grade, he talked his mother into taking him to a bookstore. David loved science fiction, and his mother had promised to buy him a particular book he had been wanting.

"Mom, here's the one I wanted. And look! They have all five books in the series. Can we buy all of them?" David asked.

"No," his mother told him. "I promised to buy you one book."

But David continued to pester her for the entire series, and she finally relented. *After all*, she thought, *you can never spoil a child with too many books*.

David didn't read all the time. He also liked to play. The Robinson family went fishing and bowling together. They also played golf, baseball, football, basketball, tennis, and Ping-Pong together.

When Mr. Robinson was not at sea, he tried to make the most of the time he had with his children. After teaching them how to play a new game, he would play with his kids for hours.

David's dad also liked to watch sports on television with his children. During and after the broadcasts, they would talk about the games they watched and discuss the rules and why things were happening the way they were. Because of this, Kim, David, and Chuck knew a lot about sports even before they played them.

While they lived in Virginia Beach, their dad taught bowling to nine- and ten-year-olds. He taught David how to hit a baseball with both his right and left hands. He served as an assistant coach when David played Little League baseball and Pee Wee football.

His parents always thought baseball was the game David played best. When he came up to bat in Little League, they would cheer for David to hit a home run, and he often did—sometimes right-handed and sometimes left-handed.

David also liked to run races. When he competed, he usually won. Afterwards, he loved to run into the house, pretend to sound a trumpet, and show his mom the newest first-place blue ribbon he had won.

When David was ten years old, he won the Virginia long-jump competition. That was a first-place blue ribbon that he was very proud of. David and his coach got to go to Kentucky to compete in the national competition. But as he was jumping in the finals, he fell. Surprisingly, he still placed second—in the nation!

When he saw his mother, though, he was reluctant to show her his ribbon. "I only won the red," he told her. But Mrs. Robinson told her son just how proud she was of him—not only because he had placed second but also because he had set such high standards for himself.

Unfortunately, not everything David did made his parents proud.

5

TEMPTED TO STEAL

One day David and Chuck wandered into a convenience store near the school bus stop. As they stood in front of a shelf full of candy, David looked around. Was anybody watching? Only four-year-old Chuck.

I could steal some of this candy, ten-year-old David thought. Then he scooped up a handful of peanut butter cups and slipped them into his pocket. Glancing around, he was sure that no one saw him do it. David breathed a sigh of relief. *That was easy!* he thought as he filled the other pocket.

David picked up a large candy bar and headed for the cash register. He tried to be casual as he placed the candy bar on the counter and handed the cashier the money.

"Son, will you step around here, please!" The man's stern voice startled David. *How could he know?* David wondered. He had no idea that his bulging pocket had given him away.

Walking around the counter and facing that man was one of the worst moments of David's life. His parents had taught him how important it is to be honest. David knew he had done something really bad—and he had been caught.

The cashier called David's mother, "You'll have to come down to the store," she told Mrs. Robinson. While the boys waited, Chuck kept telling David, "I'm going to tell! You are going to be in *so* much trouble." By the time his mother arrived, David was crying. Other shoppers, some of them friends and neighbors, watched as David confessed and apologized. Then his mom took David home and spanked him. She even spanked Chuck for going along with the crime.

David's father was at sea, so David had to wait several weeks for his dad to get home. All that time, he worried. What would his father do?

But when his dad got home, he just talked to David. He didn't spank him. Freda had already done that. He also knew David felt really bad about what he had done. Just the waiting and worrying about what would happen when his father came home had been punishment enough for David.

Perhaps one reason David had been so worried about his punishment was because he'd never forgotten an earlier incident. When David was six or seven years old, while watching television, he absentmindedly began to poke a small pocketknife into the arm of his father's leather recliner. He wasn't trying to damage the chair on purpose, he just wasn't thinking about what he was doing.

When David got up from the chair, he looked down and saw what he had done. *Uh-oh*, he thought. *I did that!*

When David's father saw the ugly holes in his favorite chair, he was angry. "For every hole in this chair, I am going to spank you once," he said.

Poor David! That was a long spanking, but he learned an important lesson about how to treat other people's property.

★

David loved doing things with his father. In fact, whenever Ambrose Robinson worked around the house, David was usually by his side.

David watched as his father repaired their family cars. First, his dad would get a Chilton manual and read the instructions. Then he and David would put on some work gloves and crawl under the car. He taught David—and himself—to do most repairs.

When he needed a Phillips-head screwdriver, his dad would send David for one. If he came back with the wrong one, his father would explain the difference and send David back for the right one.

In addition to repairing cars together, his dad bought electronic kits, and he and David put together radios and televisions by following the instructions that came with the kits.

David quickly learned to read instructions and follow them. He knew the difference between a transistor, a diode, and a capacitor. And he could identify all the tools in his dad's toolbox.

One day David was watching his father repair the family car and wondering how he had learned to do so many things. "Dad, did you go to Dad School or something?" he asked.

When David, Kim, and Chuck got home from school each day, they would find their mother's chore list on either the refrigerator or the bulletin board. Sometimes, David would cook dinner and Kim would wash the dishes. Or their mother might have instructed them to mow the lawn, trim the shrubs, vacuum the floors, or take out the garbage. Even when they were small, David's parents expected them to help out around the house.

David and his brother and sister were also expected to attend church and Bible study. As a baby, David's mom would leave him in the church nursery. But when he was three years old, he began staying with her during the services at least some of the time. If he misbehaved in church, she corrected him. She thought, *If he can't sit through a service for an hour or two, how will he sit still in kindergarten?*

Unless she had to work, Mrs. Robinson attended church every Sunday, and she always took her children with her.

When they were teenagers, David, Kim, and Chuck started asking their mother, "Do we have to go?"

"Yes," Mrs. Robinson replied. "The Lord has been good to you this week. You owe it to him. We all need the Lord. And you might learn something new."

David's mother didn't make her children go to church when they were sick. So sometimes, they would tell her that they had a headache or a stomachache. She would answer, "Okay, but sick people don't get to have any activities. If we go skating or bowling or out for ice cream later today, you won't be able to go with us." Usually the "sick" child quickly recovered and went on to church.

One November day when David was in grade school, he came home and told his mother, "The teacher wants us to bring in four cans of food for the

Thanksgiving basket. And she wants us to give her names of poor families. They'll select five names for the Thanksgiving baskets."

That afternoon, his mom was tired. She worked every day, yet she was the mother who ended up driving David and a lot of other children to all the baseball and football practices. It seemed like David, Kim, and Chuck were always bringing home notes from school asking for something.

Irritated, Mrs. Robinson told David, "Every time I turn around, it's give, give, give. This is the poor house right here. Our name needs to be in that basket."

His mother didn't mean what she had said, but David took her seriously. He put their name in the basket at school for the Thanksgiving food basket and in a similar basket at church.

David's mother was shocked when she received a phone call from the teacher. "Freda, you are trying to be slick. Why did you have David put your name in for a poor basket?"

That call was followed by another one from David's Sunday school teacher. "Freda, we caught you! David put your name in for a Thanksgiving basket. But it didn't work!"

After Mrs. Robinson assured both the callers that the family was fine, and David had simply misunderstood, she had a talk with her son. "Mama, I was only trying to help. You told me this was the poor house," he told her.

6

QUITTING THE TEAM

One day when David was eleven years old, his dad gave him his first golf lesson. They found themselves on a driving range using adult-sized clubs. To make matters worse, the clubs were made for a right-handed golfer, and David was left-handed. Just the same, David was a quick learner. With his dad telling him which club to use, David soon won a tournament for his age group.

David also continued to do well in school. As part of his sixth- and seventh-grade gifted program, he took courses in speed-reading, algebra, and advanced math at a local junior college. He was so good in math that by the time he was in junior high, his teacher was allowing him to grade papers. The teacher would drive by the Robinson house and drop off all the papers for David to work on.

One day the teacher forgot to include the answer sheet. David called and told him that it was missing. "You don't need the master sheet. You already know all the answers," his teacher told him. And he was right. David answered all the questions and graded the papers correctly.

★

In the eighth grade, David had a teacher he really didn't like. So when he brought home his first report card, he had made one A, two B's, and one C. His parents grounded David for six weeks. Until he brought home an acceptable grade report, David could not leave his house or yard after school.

David was expected to do his best, and a C was obviously not the best that David Robinson—or any Robinson—could do. David did not know any other family that took such drastic action over one low grade. But David learned that his parents would not accept less than his best.

If you had seen David Robinson's first attempt to play on an organized basketball team, you would never have guessed that he would one day be a basketball star. In junior high, David made the team but spent most of his time on the bench.

David was 5 feet, 9 inches tall—pretty good for a junior high student. And he was a good athlete. But he hadn't played much basketball at home or in the neighborhood, so he wasn't always sure what he should be doing on the court.

He went to basketball practice every day and attended all the games. But David hadn't learned any of the flashy playground moves so many of the other kids had mastered, so he was reluctant to handle the ball. While his teammates loved to dribble and drive and shoot, David preferred to play defense and not be the center of attention.

In the locker room, David also felt out of place. The other players were "cool" kids, and David was a bookworm—a "brain." At practices and in the locker room, the other guys talked about girls. David was much more interested in books. He didn't start dating girls until after he graduated from high school.

Finally, David grew tired of feeling awkward around the other players on his team. He was frustrated that he spent so much time practicing and so little time playing in games. So he went to his father. "Dad," he said, "I want to quit the basketball team. I'm not getting any playing time. They only put me in when we're twenty points up and there's two minutes left."

David and his father spent only a couple of minutes talking about it. Mr. Robinson felt that if David wanted to spend his time studying rather than playing basketball, he was not going to argue with him. "That's fine, David," his dad said. "You don't have to play."

Then David had to talk to his mother about it.

"Mom, I don't want to be a bench warmer," he told her. "It's a waste of my time."

His mother listened to David's reasons. What he had to say satisfied her.

"To be a quitter is to be a loser," David's mom responded. "But sometimes you need to quit some things. You have to be levelheaded about it. There's a thin line between quitting and being a quitter. If you can recognize the line that says, 'Quit now while you're ahead,' you'll be okay."

That was the first time David ever quit any team or activity. That basketball team went on to win the city championship, but he was never sorry he made that decision.

★

When David was fifteen years old, his dad bought a large-screen television kit. This was different from any of the other kits that he and David had put together. For one thing, this one cost a lot more— $500 or $600. Father and son had never tackled anything quite so complicated.

The Heathkit was delivered to the house while his dad was still at sea. His father had planned for them to work on it as soon as he got home. But a couple of weeks before his dad was due home, David opened the big box that had been sitting in the family den. He started putting one of the smaller boards together.

When his mother got home from work that day, Kim met her as she got out of her car. "Mom, I tried to stop him! David is in a world of trouble."

Mrs. Robinson was startled. "What happened?" she wanted to know.

"David got into that box, and he is messing with Daddy's television," Kim explained.

"David and his daddy will build that when his daddy gets back," her mother replied.

"Mom, you don't understand. He's got a whole board done."

Mrs. Robinson headed into the house to investigate, finding David in the den. Kim was right. David had opened the box and was working on it.

"David, do you know how much that kit cost?" his mother wanted to know.

"Mom, I know what I'm doing," David insisted. He kept on working.

"You had better not solder on that board unless you are absolutely sure. It will be ruined if you are wrong," his mother warned him. David was using a soldering gun, a tool that melts metal pieces together. If he soldered the wrong parts together, the whole kit would be ruined.

"Mom, you worry too much," David answered. He kept on reading the instructions and working, just like he had seen his father do with smaller kits.

When Freda went to pick up her husband at his ship, she was nervous. "Honey, don't get mad, but David put your kit together."

"Oh, I wouldn't worry about it. He knows what he's doing." David's dad was a lot calmer than his mother. And he was right!

Once at home, David's dad had a chance to look the television over. It wasn't working, but David insisted that the kit was missing a piece. His father checked and decided that David's conclusion was correct.

Mr. Robinson went to the Heathkit store and picked up the missing piece. As soon as it was in place, the new television worked. The television had a really good picture for a six-foot television screen. The Robinsons still have it in their home, and it still works well.

Some time later, David and his dad went back to the Heathkit store to make some purchases. There, he noticed a frustrated technician working on a demonstration model. David walked over to watch and began to advise him. When the man took David's advice, the problem was solved.

7

DECISION TIME

Ambrose Robinson was *not about* to buy his daughter Kimberly a moped, even though he knew how badly she wanted one. But Kim wouldn't let him forget about it. She kept talking and begged. She explained, in detail, how useful it would be. But her dad thought it would be too dangerous, and he was sure she was too young.

Finally, Freda came up with a plan. They would tell Kim that she could have a moped, but she would have to pay for it herself. The moped cost $600, and Kim made only one dollar an hour babysitting. It would take her a long time to earn that much money. Maybe by then she would lose interest. But they agreed that if she could save that much money, she would be allowed to buy it.

Her parents presented their plan to Kim, and she agreed. Then she went to work!

Six hundred dollars was a lot of babysitting. But Kim made it. She worked and saved, and finally, she bought the moped. She was so proud!

Kim rode that moped all around the neighborhood, and she took good care of it. She kept it cleaned and polished and parked in the garage out of the weather. Every now and then, she even let David take it for a ride. He loved it!

Kim kept the moped until she got her driver's license and was able to drive the car. Then she decided to give the moped to David for his birthday.

David was thrilled. What a birthday present! He rode the moped up and down the street, telling everyone he saw that the moped now belonged to him. He was convinced Kimberly was the best sister in the world.

One afternoon, several months later, Mrs. Robinson came home to find her daughter in tears.

"Mama," Kimberly cried, "David sold the moped for $90!"

Kimberly was hurt and angry. How had David dared sell the moped that had meant so much to her? And to sell it for next to nothing!

"I wouldn't have given it to him, if I'd known he didn't want it," she told her mother.

Freda went to talk to David about it. David told her that since the moped was his, he had thought he could do anything he wanted with it.

His mother thought about it. She knew the boy to whom David had sold the moped and she knew his mother. If she talked to them, she knew that she could make arrangements for David to buy the moped back. The boy who had bought it knew that the moped was worth a lot more than he had paid for it. It would only be fair for her to get the moped back for David. But what would he learn about what he had done?

David's mother made up her mind and said to him, "I am not going to ask that boy to give the moped back. I'm going to let him keep it. But your bike is broken, and your Dad and I will not fix it. We won't take you anywhere, either, so don't even ask us to drive you. From now on, you will have to walk wherever you go. And when your $90 runs out, you're on your own."

David was quickly sorry that he had sold the moped. He got very tired of walking. His sister Kimberly would have nothing to do with him for weeks.

While David was in high school, his father retired from the Navy and took a job consulting on government contracts. Mr. Robinson's new career took him to Crystal City, Virginia, near Washington, D. C., about 185 miles from their home in Virginia Beach. At first, his dad commuted to Crystal City. He would stay in an apartment near his work during the week and come home on the weekend. Finally, after a year, the Robinsons bought a house in Woodbridge, Virginia, near his job, and on October 31, 1982, the family moved to their new home.

David struggled with the decision to move. He was a senior in high school. His school was reputed to be in one of the nation's best school districts. And he had good friends in Virginia Beach. He knew what his class schedule would be. He had been looking forward to taking calculus and was signed up for several advanced classes. David told his parents he didn't want to move. Since it only seemed to make sense for him to stay behind and finish high school, they made arrangements for David to live with a family friend.

His mother cried the night they left David behind. As soon as they were gone, David knew he had made a mistake. He missed his family and wanted to live with them. But he didn't know how to tell his parents that he had changed his mind.

Each morning before school, David would call and talk to his mother. She could tell he was feeling homesick. So after two weeks, she asked David if he wanted to join the family in Woodbridge. The words were barely out of her mouth before David answered, "Yes, Ma'am!"

Freda immediately called her husband with the news.

"Why are you calling me?" Ambrose told her. "Just go get him."

David's mom called her lonely son. "Tell the guidance counselor I said to get all your papers together because you're moving. I'll be down there in three hours."

"Oh, yes, ma'am!" David answered. Before his mom arrived, David had his bags packed and his paperwork done.

"Mama," he told her, "I'm so glad you came. I missed you."

The next day, David's dad took him to register at his new school. They went first to Garfield High only a few blocks from their new home. But they found out their neighborhood had been rezoned, and David was told he needed to go to Osbourne Park High School in Mannassas, thirteen miles away.

This did not seem like good news, but they drove to Osbourne Park. That's where David met Art Payne, who became his guidance counselor and his basketball coach. Payne took one look at this 6 foot 7 inch new kid and asked David, "Why don't you try out for the basketball team?"

The rest of that day, the students kept telling David, "You've got to play basketball!" Everyone was friendly, and David didn't want to say no.

That afternoon, he watched the team practice. He even made a few shots in his stocking feet. The next day he took his physical examination and started practice with the team. The team had been practicing together for a while, but had not yet played a game.

The team had another 6-foot 7-inch player who played center. But that player had been injured, and David suddenly became the team's starting center.

In the first game of the season, David scored 14 points and grabbed 14 rebounds. Coach Payne could see that David had lots of raw talent. He had never coached another big man who was such a natural at handling the ball. But it was obvious David had never played enough to develop his basketball instincts.

Coach Payne asked a former college basketball center to come to practices and work with David on fundamentals. Since David was a quick learner, he developed rapidly during the season. David averaged 14 points per game and made the All-Area and All-District teams.

But basketball was nothing more than a game to David. With college just around the corner, he had a future to plan. And he never expected basketball to be part of it.

8

BASKETBALL OR EDUCATION?

Because he hadn't played basketball until his senior year of high school, David was surprised so many college recruiters showed an interest in him. But the combination of his size and impressive high school academic record (plus a score of 1320 on the SAT) drew a lot of attention. Harvard, Holy Cross, and George Mason University all expressed interest.

But part way through his senior basketball season, Paul Evans, the basketball coach at the Naval Academy in Annapolis, Maryland, received a phone call from a Navy officer who lived in David's hometown. "There's a big kid playing for Osbourne Park," he said. "You need to come down and see him."

So Coach Evans drove down to Northern Virginia to take a look. "David was a skinny kid who could run," he remembered, "but he couldn't do much else." Coach Evans wasn't very impressed.

However, Evans followed David's performance for the remainder of the season. He saw enough improvement to convince him that in time David might become a decent college athlete. He could tell David was interested in the Academy.

"David wanted a good education," Evans said. "His father had a career in the Navy, so I think the idea of becoming a naval officer appealed to him. The education certainly did."

Coach Evans had David figured right—at least about one thing. David was actually more interested in the quality of education he would receive than he was the school's basketball program. All his life he had figured he would become an engineer or some kind of scientist. If being good enough to stick a ball through a hoop and tall enough to keep others from doing it got him a college scholarship—great! But David was much more concerned about getting an education that would prepare him for his future career.

Like Coach Evans, David's father also had watched the remarkable improvement in his son's basketball skills. He had begun to think David had a real future in basketball. If that were true, there would be a serious advantage in David going somewhere besides a United States Military Academy where he would be required to spend five years in the Navy after graduation.

When Ambrose Robinson visited the Virginia Military Institute with David, he was convinced it would be the perfect school for his son. VMI offered both military school discipline and an excellent engineering department. The small campus seemed like a great environment for learning. David's dad liked the coaches. He was impressed with the fact that they ran a basketball program that would enable his son to go right into the pros after graduation.

David liked VMI well enough. But he was practically awestruck when he came home from a weekend visit to the Naval Academy. "Wow, Mom!" he exclaimed. "The lab set up is better than any college I've visited. They have so much equipment I couldn't believe it. But I just can't make up my mind."

"David," his mother said, "Annapolis sounds wonderful. I like the Naval Academy. But the question is, which school do you like best?"

"Dad likes VMI," he replied.

"David," his mother told him, "Go where *you* want to go, not where I want you to go or where your daddy wants you to go. You have to decide which school you think would be best for you."

David thought he knew the answer already. "Probably the Naval Academy. Mom, you should see their labs!"

But David still hadn't given the schools or his parents his final answer. "I was still torn," he says. "I knew it needed to be my decision, but part of me wanted my parents to make it for me. Or at least tell me what they thought I should do. They kept saying they wanted me to decide, but I could tell they each had their own ideas."

David had always tried to be an obedient son who never wanted to disappoint his dad. So when his father pressed his son to tell him what he was thinking, David told him he thought VMI would be a great school. His father heard, or thought he heard, David saying, "I guess I'll go to VMI."

So Mr. Robinson phoned VMI and three of their coaches drove down to sign the skinny, raw basketball recruit who'd only played one year of high school ball. The VMI recruiters were in the den talking to David and his dad when Mrs. Robinson came downstairs and walked into the room. "What's going on?" she asked.

"These are the people from VMI coming to sign David," Mr. Robinson told her.

"No, they're not!" Mrs. Robinson said.

David's father and the VMI coaches were surprised. They thought the matter was settled. Everyone turned to look at David.

After a long and awkward silence, David told them, "I'm going to the Naval Academy." Then he thanked the men for coming.

After the disappointed VMI coaches had gone, Mrs. Robinson asked her son, "You're not going to Navy because I liked it are you?"

"Mom," he told her, "It's the best place for *me*."

"You need to be sure you're going there for the right reason," she said.

"I am," he replied.

Mrs. Robinson felt like dancing. But she didn't because she realized she needed to cheer up her husband. "The education he will get at the Naval Academy will far outweigh the five years of quick money he might make playing basketball. Besides, basketball is secondary."

"You're right," Mr. Robinson agreed. He'd always believed that education was more important than sports. He had often told his children so. He was less disappointed than he was embarrassed about inviting the VMI recruiters to come before he really understood what David wanted to do. He always did believe the final decision was his son's to make. After all, David was the one who would have to live with the choice.

David wasn't so sure he'd made the right decision on the hot July day in 1983 when he reported to the Naval Academy in Annapolis. Starting the day dressed in jeans and a casual shirt, David spent most of the morning with his new classmates—filling out forms, receiving uniforms, and finally getting dormitory assignments. "I remember standing in all these different lines waiting to go to all these different places," he says. "It was one of the longest days of my life."

And it would get longer. At the end of the afternoon, the new midshipmen were finally sworn in. Then they were sworn at.

"Suddenly, all the upperclassmen started yelling at us and telling us where to go," David recalled. "Earlier in the day, they'd been polite. But once we were sworn in, they weren't polite at all. I remember all these people yelling at me and thinking, *What have I gotten myself into? Was it a mistake to come here?*" Sleep didn't come easily that first night.

The physical demands were also tough. To start with, all midshipmen were expected to swim one hundred meters—four lengths of the pool. David couldn't make it. So he was assigned to a swimming class where he had to swim for forty minutes at a time. He also had to dive off a tower thirty feet high. It would take him a while to conquer his fear and learn to make the dive without thinking.

For a long time David wondered about the wisdom of his decision. "That first month I was at school, I didn't know if I was going to cut it," he admits. If the physical stuff didn't kill him, the academic demands threatened to do him in.

"Going in, I felt pretty good about my qualifications," he said. "But almost immediately it hit me, *Wow! There are a lot of really smart people here.* It seemed like everyone I talked to was first or second in his high school class and had scored 1500 or more on their SATs.

"Suddenly, I felt like I was down at the bottom of the barrel. I knew I was going to have to work harder than I had in high school just to keep up."

Would he be able to do it? After feeling so convinced that Navy was the place for him, David began to seriously question his college decision. *Maybe I made a big mistake,* he thought. He seriously began to think about quitting.

NAVAL ACADEMY DISCIPLINE

David honestly didn't know if he could handle the hazing and the demanding physical conditioning the freshmen "plebes" had to endure to prove they were tough enough to become Navy officers.

The daily schedule was bad enough. David and the other midshipmen all had to get up early, shower, shave, dress, eat breakfast and report for daily marching drills at 7:30 A.M. Then they attended four hours of classes, ate lunch, and went back to classes until late afternoon. In the evening, they ate dinner, endured marching drills, and then spent time studying before bedtime.

The classes themselves were tough—thermodynamics, navigation, advanced calculus, physics, computer science, electrical engineering, weapons, history of science and technology, contemporary American literature, advanced computer programming, celestial navigation, advanced numerical analysis, computer data structures, partial differential equations, and economic geography. The homework load nearly overwhelmed him that first term. "Most days we had too much," David says. "The rest of the time we had *way* too much."

"In high school I had taken things for granted," he says. "My classes had always been easy. I didn't have to study for them. Then I got to the Naval Academy and I didn't have time to do anything else. Wow! There was so much work to do. I had to focus. But I soon realized how much stronger that was making me as a student and as a person."

The lessons his parents had taught came back to him. And he decided to stick it out.

David shared a room with Carl "Hootie" Liebert in Bancroft hall where 137 other midshipmen also lived. The dorm had no TVs, only one phone, and plebes were never allowed to leave campus to shop, see a movie, or even grab a McDonald's hamburger except on special occasions. Even then they had to ask for and receive official permission. So there weren't a lot of options on campus to distract the students from their studies.

David needed all of the focus and discipline he could get. Once the basketball team began working out, he would be facing all the academic challenges the other students had, and he would need to fit daily practice into an already packed schedule. Then he would have to find ways to keep up his class work while playing a thirty-game basketball season with evening and weekend road trips all over the country.

David planned to play basketball, but he wasn't at all sure how seriously he would take the game. After all, he'd only played one year in high school. "I figured basketball would just be an outlet for me—a change of pace from studies," David says.

But basketball at the college level proved to be a tougher challenge and a bigger distraction than David had anticipated. From his first practice scrimmages, Coach Evans had David line up against the team's best player, 6-foot, 7-inch Vernon Butler, who was nicknamed Captain Crunch for his physical style of play. He and David also battled each other in rebounding drills.

"I got beat up every day in practice," David recalls. "I caught a lot of elbows and spent a lot of time protecting my nose. The game just didn't come naturally to me, so basketball seemed like more work than fun."

Keeping up with academics was also more difficult than he'd expected. "You get out of practice and you're tired," he says. "You wake up in the morning and you're already tired from what you did the day before."

Paul Evans demanded and expected total dedication from his players. But David just didn't share his enthusiasm for the game. Pete Herrman, the assistant coach David's first three years, says it was obvious that basketball wasn't that important to David. "There wasn't much he liked about his freshman year, including practice. Later he told me he would sit in his math class sixth period and say to himself, 'Oh, brother, I have to go to basketball practice today.'"

David got so tired playing basketball and trying to keep up with his studies that he kept falling asleep in class. He even slept standing up. It got so bad that Naval Academy officials thought he might have a medical problem. When David broke his hand boxing in a physical education class, they realized what was happening. The x-rays of David's broken hand showed a significant gap in his bones—David was still growing. In fact, he was growing so fast, his body needed extra rest to keep up.

So the broken bone turned out not to be bad news at all for the Navy basketball coaches and doctors. In fact, the doctor who called David's parents about his injury was excited about what they'd discovered.

"David will probably be a seven-footer," he told them. If that were true, it would indeed be amazing news for the team.

Because of the close quarters aboard ships and submarines, the Navy wanted most of its officers to be less than 6-feet 6-inches tall. A small percentage of each Academy class could be as tall as 6 feet 8 inches but no taller. At 6 feet 7-1/2 inches, David had been just under the upper limit when he took his entrance physical in February of his senior year. But once accepted, midshipmen can't become ineligible if they grow. And grow David did. He was 6 feet 9 inches by the time he enrolled, and now the x-rays indicated that he would soon be more than 7 feet tall.

The coaches had hoped David would become a decent small forward. They were absolutely thrilled at the prospect of him growing into the big-time center Navy had never had.

However, they soon began to wonder if those dreams would ever come true. David had an unimpressive freshman season. He missed the first four games because of his broken hand. When he did come back, he wasn't a starter and didn't play much. He averaged 7.6 points after playing about 13 minutes a game.

Yet Coach Evans remained convinced of David's potential. He liked the way such a big kid could get up and down the court. But he didn't like the fact that David seemed lazy in practice. He couldn't figure out how to motivate him.

Some of the other players on the team must have seen David's potential as well. They kidded him and called him "Country" when they learned he'd never flown in an airplane or been inside a hotel or a bar.

But they quickly noticed how graceful and athletic he was. His roommate Hootie Leibert recalls a required three-week course in gymnastics. "Dave was so big I didn't think he could do it. But after the rest of us looked bad, he gets up on the parallel bars and starts making these fancy moves and doing all sorts of stuff. It only took him a week to do everything required to get an A in the course.

"He was so good at everything, it was disgusting," Hootie says. "I wished there was just one sport I could beat him in. He could shoot a great round of golf, and he played tennis well. I thought maybe I could take him at squash since the court is so little. But he beat me at that too."

As the season progressed, David's basketball skills steadily improved. He played well enough to be named rookie of the year in the conference. Navy's basketball team won twenty games for the first time in the school's history. By the end of the year, David had grown to 6 feet 10 inches tall.

The coaches were more convinced than ever that he had the potential to be something special on the basketball court. But head coach Paul Evans grew even more frustrated that David didn't seem to understand or appreciate his great physical talent. The coaches hadn't yet found a good strategy for motivating him.

Evans had really tried to push David in practice, working him hard and yelling at him a lot whenever he thought his big man was slacking off. While there had been steady improvement during the season, there were times the coach felt his freshman center just tuned him out.

Not knowing what else to do, Evans finally went to David's father. "How can I motivate your son?" he asked. Mr. Robinson wasn't sure either.

Finally the coach called David into his office. He told the young player he might someday make a lot of money as a professional basketball player if he would work harder to develop his game.

David wasn't convinced. He still wasn't sure how badly he even wanted to play basketball.

10

TALLEST PLAYER IN
NAVY HISTORY

David did however begin working with Navy's strength coach, lifting weights and running to stay in shape during the off-season. He also spent the summer playing against outstanding college and pro stars in the Washington Urban Coalition League.

By the time he returned to Annapolis the fall of his sophomore year, David had developed an outstanding shooting touch. He seemed quicker and more agile despite the fact that he had added 25 or 30 pounds of muscle and had grown to 6 feet 11 inches tall.

The coaches were more excited than ever about David's physical development. He was now the tallest player in Navy history. If they could find a way to get him to make the most of his skills, they believed their team could actually improve on last year's 24-8 record.

That David hadn't played much in high school was turning out to be an advantage. Coach Evans actually liked the fact that his young center was still learning the game. "It was like coaching a ninth or tenth grader," he says. Because David hadn't already played for five or six years, he didn't have a lot of bad habits on the floor that he needed to break. "Plus it's a lot easier to teach a kid with great intelligence, which David had."

Still, David's performance was not impressive during the first couple of games that season. Then in game three against American University, he broke out for 29 points and 11 rebounds, leading the way for an impressive 84-68 Navy win. After that game American's coach said about David, "He's one of the top big men in the east."

A few days later, David really caught fire at a tournament in Illinois. Against Southern Illinois University, he scored 31 points and snatched 13 rebounds against SIU's 6-foot, 11-inch center. And the next night against Western Illinois, he looked even better with 37 points and 17 rebounds.

David couldn't believe what he'd done. "It was the first time I got an idea of what I could do," he says.

Hootie Liebert remembers that after the Western Illinois game, David turned to him and said, "Wow! I can play!"

In four games that week, including the two games of the tournament, David scored a total of 115 points, grabbed 52 rebounds, and won the Saluki Shootout MVP award. David wasn't the only one impressed with his performances. Navy's opponents just couldn't stop him. He was too quick for their big men to cover and too tall for the little guys. He outran the guards down the floor on fast breaks and then out-jumped the frontcourt guys for rebounds and dunks.

The media noticed too. Newspapers and magazines all over the country ran stories about Navy's amazing center. *Sports Illustrated* named him Player of the Week. To David's surprise, it seemed he'd suddenly become a big-time player.

"I'd never thought of myself that way," he admits. "In high school, basketball was just something I experimented with." Now, at last, David realized he had the potential to be good—if he worked at it. Yet he still frustrated his coaches when he told the media, "If I don't become a big star, it isn't that big a deal. I still play to have fun."

After the Illinois tournament, the Navy team went almost four weeks without any games to give players the chance to study and take final exams. David tried to focus on schoolwork, but it was during this time that sportswriters in various papers began to speculate that he might consider leaving Navy at the end of the school year.

The experts were saying he was good enough to play professional ball. And if he transferred to another school, he wouldn't have to do his five years of military service. He could go to the NBA as soon as he graduated.

So, naturally, reporters began asking David about his plans. "When people bring up pro basketball to me, I laugh," he told them. "I don't think of myself that way. Basketball is just one of the things I do." People were talking about him transferring, but he wasn't considering it. In fact, he said if people hadn't started asking him about it, "I never would have thought about it at all."

But the flood of speculation forced him to think about it. Almost every day someone reminded him by writing about how much money he could make as a professional basketball player. The idea of making a good living playing a game was tempting. He admitted that when people talked about playing basketball for hundreds of thousands of dollars a year, "You can't help but have it on your mind."

He also told interviewers, "Maybe I don't think I'm as good as other people seem to think I am. Right now I don't see any reason to leave Navy. It's a tough place, but I'm happy here."

When the season resumed in January, David led Navy to ten straight victories. The midshipman began attracting their biggest crowds ever. It seemed everyone turned out to watch David Robinson play. They were seldom disappointed.

Navy finished the season with an impressive 22-5 record. Then they won three post-season games in a row to take the East Coast Athletic Conference South—the first Navy team since 1960 to be invited to play in the NCAA tournament. They defeated a favored Louisiana State University team in the opening round before finally being eliminated by Maryland. It was an incredible accomplishment for the team and an impressive achievement for David.

Finishing the season with 756 points, David broke a school record, which had stood for thirty-one years. David also set Navy records for field goals, 30-point games, and rebounding. He received all conference honors and was voted ECAC South Player of the Year.

By the time the season ended, David was 7 feet, 1 inch tall. There was no longer any question that he was a legitimate pro prospect. He was forced to make a decision about his future.

If he came back to Annapolis the next fall for his junior year, he would be expected to graduate and then required to serve out his five years in the Navy. Did he want to risk delaying or losing a possible NBA career? Or should he transfer to a big basketball school, lose one year of college eligibility, but work on his game and try to improve his basketball potential and his future earnings?

David knew this was a big decision. Notre Dame, UCLA, Kentucky, Georgetown, and Indiana would be glad to take him.

He discussed the pros and cons with his parents a number of times over the next few months. They talked to the Naval Academy superintendent who suggested that David might not be required to serve all five years. He hinted that because David was so tall he might not have to serve at all, or his term of service might be limited to two years. But he couldn't offer any guarantees.

There were no guarantees if he transferred either. Yes, it could mean millions of dollars in just two or three years. But NCAA rules would require him to sit out a season, and who knew how much or how well he might play once he became eligible.

David told Coach Evans, "I like basketball and it's a challenge. But it is just one part of my life. If I have to, I can live without it."

David remembers what he was thinking at the time. "My first two years at the Naval Academy had been a great experience. The education was obviously top notch. And I enjoyed the people, going out on the ships during the summer, and getting that experience. The demands were making me a better, more disciplined person. And I needed that."

He was a little afraid that if he transferred to another school where no one required or expected him to go to class every day, he might be tempted to blow off his academics. "I knew the standard the

Navy held me to was something I really needed and now appreciated. When I was on the campus at Annapolis, I felt almost isolated from the world. I could concentrate and learn there. There was no partying. No fraternities or sororities. No social causes to get involved in. No distractions. Just time to study and get your work done."

It was a tough choice—one that kept him lying awake at night staring at the ceiling of his dorm room. If he stayed at the Academy and graduated, he'd be guaranteed a job in the Navy that paid $20,000 a year plus food, housing, and travel. He'd probably be twenty-seven years old before he got a chance to play in the NBA; his skills might be too rusty by then.

David says, "I knew the decision could mean a lot of money. And people think you will automatically be happy if you have a lot of money. But I didn't necessarily believe that was true."

When David finally made his decision, he asked a Navy spokesman to read this statement to reporters: "The Academy has been good for me, and I want the chance to receive a degree from here. Pro ball? I guess I still have a hard time visualizing myself playing at that level with all those great players. I want to improve on what we accomplished this year. Everyone is saying I'm great, but who can you listen to? I'm in control. I'm doing what I want to do. I have no regrets. I came here for academics, but all my goals got cloudy. The press confused me a lot. Basketball came so fast. It really just came together this year. I'm still in my early stages. I don't know how much basketball means to me right now."

That was it. David had made his decision. He had chosen academics over sports.

He never anticipated the reaction. He was praised in speeches and editorials all over America for his character. People were more impressed than ever. Here was a young man who chose commitment, loyalty, learning, and national service over celebrity and wealth.

Ironically, it made him more famous than ever. He tried to downplay what he'd done by saying he'd merely listened to his heart. His experience with the Navy had been good so far, "so I went with the flow. Fulfilling my commitment simply felt like the right thing to do."

Indeed, it eventually turned out to be the right thing for David Robinson to do—in more ways than one. But there would be times over the next few years when he couldn't help but wonder if he'd made a mistake.

11

"THE ADMIRAL"

David felt like he was playing basketball in an oven. The sweat dripped off his nose, his chin, and his elbows. He could feel it rolling down his arms, his legs, and his back. It was 105 degrees and his United States' teammates never seemed to let up in their preparations for an international tournament event called the Jones Cup. David was impressed by the level of commitment he was witnessing. Here were some of the best college players in the country, "and these guys were busting it every day," David says. "They never wanted to stop playing. It was kind of inspiring." He was getting a glimpse of what it took to be one of the best, and the experience gave him increased confidence.

Back at the Naval Academy the following fall, his teammates noticed a change in his attitude.

His friend and roommate Hootie Liebert told reporters, "David's talking about how he can't wait to practice. I've never heard him say that before."

Experts ranked Navy among the top 20 teams in the country in a pre-season poll. Many people were calling David the nation's best college center. Coach Evans continued to believe he could be—but only if he started working harder. David still had a tendency to let up and coast unless his competition really pushed him.

When his coach tried to push him, David resented it. Evans was an old-fashioned screamer. He seldom had an encouraging word. It wasn't unusual to hear a stream of curse words. The Navy coach could swear like a sailor.

One day when Coach Evans thought David was slacking off in practice, he blew up, pointed at the door, and told him, "Get out of the gym!" He kicked his star out of practice.

David left. But he was more mad than motivated. He figured, *The coach is playing mind games with me. It may work with other guys, but it's not going to work with me.* He thought Coach Evans was acting like a jerk.

David's father knew his son didn't appreciate being yelled at, but he felt on occasion it may have helped. "There were probably times," Mr. Robinson says, "when David buckled down and tried harder in order to prove something to his coach. He would think, *I'll show him!* and then he did."

As a junior in the 1985-86 season, David averaged 22.7 points a game and led the nation with 13.0 rebounds and 5.9 blocks a game. He set NCAA records for blocked shots in a game, season, and career. He was named to numerous All-America teams and made Player of the Year in his conference again. He became such a commanding presence on Navy's basketball court that he was nicknamed "The Admiral" and "The Aircraft Carrier."

Navy made the NCAA tournament for the second year in a row. They won handily in the first round, then faced a talented Syracuse team that boasted two future first-round NBA draft picks— Rony Seikaly and Dwayne "Pearl" Washington. David scored 35 points, hauled down 11 rebounds, blocked 7 shots and held Seikaly to just 4 points in what was a huge upset win for Navy.

In their next game, David scored the winning basket with six seconds left in the game. Navy defeated Cleveland State 71-70. One more win and the surprising Middies would be going to the Final Four. But Duke squelched that dream and ended Navy's incredible tournament run by easily winning the next game. For David it was such a disappointing end to a promising season that he complained. He accused the team of playing like a bunch of wimps and refused to talk to the press for several weeks.

Neither his teammates nor his coach took offense at his criticism. They saw it as a sign that David was caring more about basketball than he ever had before.

The summer before his senior year, David played on the U. S. National Basketball team in the World Championships held in Madrid, Spain. Once again he rose to the challenge of playing alongside and against some of the best competitors in the world as he led the U. S. to a win over the Soviets in the first American World Championship performance since 1954. David also spent two weeks in Hawaii that summer on naval duty, serving aboard an American aircraft carrier.

When he returned to Annapolis from all his travels that fall, David received encouraging news. Napolean McCallum, Navy's star running back, had been selected by the Los Angeles Raiders in the National Football League's draft the previous spring. When Napolean was stationed in Long Beach, California, not far from the Raiders' training camp, the Navy had given him permission to play football with the Raiders on Sundays. If McCallum could play football, that meant perhaps David would be given the chance to play part-time for an NBA team while he was completing his required military service.

David already knew he would be stationed at some naval base because he was too tall to serve aboard ship after he graduated. A week's assignment the previous summer aboard a submarine with six-foot ceilings and tiny living quarters convinced David and his superiors that he couldn't be expected to live constantly hunched over. One training flight folded into the cockpit of a Navy fighter plane proved he couldn't fly either. Shore duty it would have to be.

Meanwhile, he had one more season of college basketball to look forward to. Coach Evans had taken a job at the University of Pittsburgh, so his assistant Pete Herrmann took over at Navy. David thought that was a good change. There were occasions during his senior season when David realized he might have pushed a little harder with Evans yelling at him and may have even missed the tongue-lashings. But for the most part, David related better to Herrmann's quieter and more positive style as he slowly learned how to motivate himself. He usually wanted to work in order to please his new coach. He was now enjoying basketball so much and playing so well that the idea of joining the NBA seemed more appealing than ever. He found it tougher and tougher not knowing if the Navy would require him to serve five years or two years after graduation.

"Last year I was up in the air about the pros," he admitted to the press. "But, yes, I want to play now. God gave me the height and ability to play, and I want to—very much. If I had known two years ago that I would feel this way now, I might have made a different decision and not stayed here."

David began the season with a bang, pouring in 36 points in an opening loss to North Carolina State and then leading Navy to a one-point overtime win over Michigan State in which he scored a new career high of 43 points. But as the season progressed, David found it difficult to concentrate on basketball or his classes. He had learned that the Navy was in the process of making a final decision regarding his length of service. The question had stirred up a lot of debate around the country. So he worried that the Navy might make an example of him and insist on a five-year commitment.

But on January 9, 1987, Navy Secretary John Lehman announced that David would have to serve two years after graduation. During that time, he would be allowed to play in the 1987 Pan American Games and the 1988 Summer Olympics. After he completed his two years of active duty, he would have to serve four years in the Naval Reserve, which would involve three weeks of training each summer.

Relieved, David went out and celebrated the Navy's decision by scoring 45 points and grabbing 21 rebounds in his team's next game against James Madison. He went on to complete another impressive season, leading the nation again in blocked shots, while ranking third in scoring and fourth in rebounding. He became the first college player ever to combine 2,500 career points, 1,300 rebounds and 60 percent shooting from the floor. He was named to every All-America team after setting 33 Navy records and launching the Middies to another NCAA playoff appearance.

Unfortunately, Navy drew the highly ranked Michigan Wolverines in the opening round of the NCAA East Regional in Charlotte, North Carolina. The fans stood and clapped when it was announced that David had won the Naismith Award as College Player of the Year. And then he really gave them something to cheer about.

Number 50 dazzled everyone in the building by scoring 50 points that night—a career high. The fact that the rest of Navy's team was no match for the super-talented Michigan squad took nothing away from David's performance.

The score wasn't close when Coach Herrmann took his star center out of the game with two seconds left—just in case anyone wanted to applaud his effort. Everyone did. The fans' standing ovation went on for several minutes as, one by one, the Michigan players ran over to shake his hand and his Navy teammates jumped off their chairs to bear hug him.

David Robinson's spectacular college career was over.

12

DRAFTED BY THE SPURS

After Navy was eliminated from the NCAA tournament, David returned to Annapolis and worked hard to catch up on his schoolwork. His grade point average had dropped during his senior year. "My mother is all over me because of that," he said.

There was good news and bad news that spring about his professional basketball prospects. The experts said he was certain to be the first player chosen in the 1987 NBA draft in June. They agreed he was by far the most talented player available. And even if he could only play part-time for the first couple of years, most teams still wanted him.

That was the good news.

The bad news was that the new Secretary of the Navy felt being an officer was a 24-hour-a-day job. He did not want Navy athletes to play professional sports until they completed their military service. That meant David wouldn't be able to join the NBA, even part-time, until his two-year commitment was over.

But even that bad news turned out to be good for David. Since he couldn't play for two years anyway, he wouldn't have to play for the first team to draft him. If for some reason he didn't like the team or wasn't willing to accept their contract, he could turn down their offer and go into the draft again the following year. If he didn't sign with the second team to draft him, he would only have to wait until his two-year service commitment was up, and he would be a free agent, able to sign with any team he wanted. He could choose to wait for a bidding war to see which team would pay him the most money. The Navy might not let him play pro ball for two years, but when it came to the future, he was suddenly very much in the driver's seat. In two years he could be playing with Michael Jordan's Bulls, Magic Johnson's Lakers, Larry Bird's Celtics, or any other player or team he might choose.

When the NBA held their draft lottery on May 17, the San Antonio Spurs won the first choice in the annual June draft and immediately announced their intention to choose David. "He's a terrific athlete," said the Spurs general manager. "When he gets with better players, he'll be even better."

Three days later, David and 1,021 of his classmates gathered in the Halsey Field House in Annapolis for graduation. One by one, thirty-six Navy companies walked to the podium. When it came his turn, David shook hands and received his diploma in mathematics and computer science from George Bush, then vice president and future president of the United States. When the last midshipman received his degree, the graduates all shouted "Beat Army!" and sailed their hats toward the sky.

Two weeks later, newly commissioned Ensign David Robinson received his orders. He was to report for duty on June 19 at Kings Bay Submarine Base in Georgia where he would serve as Assistant Resident Officer in Charge of Construction. For supervising the building of docks and service facilities for submarines, the Navy would pay him $315.23 a week.

On June 22, the San Antonio Spurs used their first pick in the NBA draft to select Ensign Robinson. They were willing to pay him millions of dollars now if he would agree to report for duty in Texas in two years to help them rebuild their basketball franchise.

David was actually in Washington, D.C., visiting with Vice President Bush at the White House and playing in a celebrity golf tournament with entertainer Bob Hope on the day of the draft. He was still out on the course when he officially heard the news that the Spurs had drafted him.

"Will you play for the Spurs?" the reporters wanted to know.

David pointed out that he already had a job. So he wasn't ready to make any decision right away. He told the reporters that he planned to visit San Antonio, meet people, look around, learn about the Spurs organization, and then make up his mind. He said the Spurs would need to convince him they were committed to improving their team, that the players were happy there, and that their fans would come out and support the team.

Later that summer, David and a bunch of other College All-Stars played for Team USA in the Pan American Games held that year in Indianapolis. The Americans expected to dominate. They'd won forty-seven times and lost only twice while winning the championship eight out of nine times since those games began.

When he didn't play particularly well until the semi-finals against Puerto Rico, everyone was asking what was wrong with David Robinson. He felt he was in shape, but he admitted, "Kings Bay is a small town, and there is nowhere within an hour's drive that I can play competitive basketball."

In the final against Brazil, David got in foul trouble early. The Brazilians hung with the U.S. until David came back in and quickly fouled out of the contest. Then Brazil surged ahead to win the game and capture the gold medal. "This is far worse than losing to Duke in the NCAA tournament," David admitted to *The Washington Post*. "Our Pan American team was absolutely expected to win and didn't. . . . One of the worst feelings an athlete can have is knowing his teammates need him and not being able to do anything about it."

The bitter taste of defeat was washed away in September when he finally made his first visit to San Antonio. What an experience!

The Spurs spent $16,000 just to charter a private jet to pick up David's parents and his brother Chuck, along with David's two agents in Washington, D.C. Then they flew to Jacksonville, Florida, to pick up David.

When they landed in San Antonio, seven hundred screaming fans met the plane. Chuck Robinson, who looks a lot like his older brother but is several inches shorter, stepped out of the plane first. The crowd cheered wildly—though some of them must have been thinking 7 feet wasn't nearly as tall as they thought it was. They were quickly reassured, however, when David ducked his head and stepped through the plane's door behind his brother.

A number of dignitaries made presentations. David said a few words to the crowd, as many of them chanted "David! David! David!" and waved signs with messages such as "Say yes! David" and

"Pretty Please?" After a short press conference, the entire family was whisked away to the city's nicest hotel, where they were given the biggest suites with bedrooms, dining rooms, and even living rooms with fireplaces.

Some of the Spurs players and officials took the Robinsons to a fancy dinner. The next morning the Spurs' bosses and the mayor took them on a helicopter tour of the city, and then to the city's most prestigious country club for lunch and a round of golf. That night, there was another elegant dinner at a French restaurant and a boat ride along the city's famous Riverwalk.

The following day, David met with the Spur officials one more time. He made no promises. But he told everyone how great it felt to be wanted and how impressed he was with the city. "I just need some time to mull over my decision," he told them.

Some people figured David would hold out until he could sign with the Lakers or the Celtics. But after just a few weeks, he gave his agents permission to see what kind of contract San Antonio had in mind. When he heard their offer, he told his friend and old roommate Hootie Liebert, "They have done everything to make me happy. They have been honest and fair. How can I turn them down?"

On November 6, 1987, David and his parents flew to San Antonio, where five hundred fans watched and cheered as he signed his contract at the HemisFair Arena. The contract made David the highest paid athlete in team sports—$26 million for eight years, plus $2 million immediately just for signing.

Now David and the city of San Antonio had to be content to wait for his professional basketball career to begin—after he finished his obligation to the Navy. In the meantime, David confessed to a *Washington Post* reporter that it seemed kind of strange to him. "I'm living in two different worlds right now. One world I rule. It's all there on a silver platter for me. People want to give me an incredible amount of money to play a game—something I enjoy. That boggles my mind.

"In the other world, I'm at the bottom of the totem pole. I might be asked to run out and get coffee for people. The whole situation is teaching me a lot. I'm learning about power and restraint."

Later he would add that it was strange living a normal life on a naval base. "I would go to NBA things—go to the All-Star game, for instance, where everyone was treated special—then come back to the base, where guys were going to the supermarket with their families, working jobs, doing all the normal things people do. I had a foot in both worlds."

"Tell me one thing," David would say to his friends after he came back from one of his outings in the world of celebrity. "Tell me if I ever change, if my head ever starts to get bigger."

But David got a real dose of humility the next year when he went to the Olympic Trials. His job hadn't given him much time to work out, and for almost a year there had been no chance to compete against top-notch basketball players. David's skills were so rusty that a lot of people again wondered what was wrong with him.

When he averaged only 12.8 points and 6.8 rebounds a game during the Olympics themselves, and especially after the coach failed to play him in the deciding minutes of the semi-final loss to the Soviet Union, more people began to question both David's skills and his commitment to basketball. Would he even be able to play at the professional level after another year away from the game?

David had his own doubts. For a long time, he blamed himself for his U.S. team ending up with a bronze rather than a gold medal.

Would he disappoint the people in San Antonio too?

13

FAME AND FORTUNE

O n May 19, 1989, the United States Navy gave
Lieutenant (Junior Grade) David Robinson his
official discharge from active duty. The time had
finally come to begin his professional basketball
career. Many people remembered his disappointing
performances in the Pan American and Olympic
games. If he couldn't lead his American teams to
victories in competitions that the U.S. had tradi-
tionally dominated, they asked, how could he be
expected to succeed in the NBA against the best
competition in the world.

David heard the comments and remembered
his own bitter disappointment against international competition. That made him even more
determined to fulfill his potential and reward the
faith the San Antonio Spurs had shown in him.

With no more college classes to attend and no other job to take his time, David Robinson was, for the first time in his life, ready to concentrate all of his attention and energy on basketball. How good could he be? After two years of waiting and wondering, he was ready to find out.

David began to get into shape and tune up his game. Then he silenced some of the critics by dominating the summer pro leagues in Texas and Southern California. He wowed his teammates and coaches during training camp and more than held his own in the pre-season exhibition games against other NBA teams.

Anticipation began to build. David Robinson literally became the talk of the town in San Antonio, Texas. In the two years since the Spurs signed him, the team had won only 52 games and lost 112. They had just changed owners, and only three players were back from the previous year's team. Clearly, everyone was counting on David Robinson to turn the tide for the Spurs franchise and transform the image of professional sports in the city.

November 4, 1989, finally arrived. "The Admiral" would make his NBA debut against the Los Angeles Lakers.

David felt the pressure. He was so nervous he threw up in the locker room before the game. But soon after the tip-off, David took a pass in the lane, leaped into the air with his back to the basket and slam-dunked the ball over his head. The crowd roared.

He proceeded to lead his team by scoring 23 points and hauling down a game-high 17 rebounds to propel the once hapless Spurs to a 106-98 victory over the Lakers. His performance prompted a defeated Magic Johnson to say after the game, "Some rookies are never really rookies. Robinson is one of them."

With the Admiral in command, the Spurs won 12 of their first 17 games. The same experts who'd wondered how he would play after two years away from the game called him one of the premier centers in the NBA—right up there with Patrick Ewing and Hakeem Olajuwon. Some NBA people even compared him to the legendary Celtic center Bill Russell, "only a better athlete" with "more offense." Other commentators were predicting, "He's going to be the best center to ever play the game." His own coach, Larry Brown, called him "the best player of that size I've ever seen."

The longer the season went on, the bigger the impression David Robinson made. He was named to the All-Star game and was a unanimous pick for NBA Rookie of the Year while averaging 24.3 points, 12.0 rebounds, and 3.9 blocks a game. The 1989-90 Spurs won 35 more games than they had the previous year—the biggest one-year turn-around in league history.

In David's second year as a professional, the NBA reported more Robinson merchandise sold than for any other player except Michael Jordan. In one year, he'd become a superstar with a national following.

He was the only NBA player to place in the top ten in four statistical categories. The top vote-getter for the West All-Star Team, he was also named All-NBA First Team, All-NBA Defensive Team, and came in third in the voting for Most Valuable Player behind Michael Jordan and Magic Johnson. As a team, the Spurs disappointed their fans after winning their division in the regular season, but losing to Golden State in the first round of the playoffs.

Very few people blamed David. He obviously did more than his part for the Spurs and was quickly establishing himself as one of the best players in the history of the game.

He had more money, fame, and success than he'd ever dreamed about. He was young, smart, good-looking, and incredibly rich. He had five fancy cars and two beautiful homes. He went out with gorgeous women. People were always telling him how great he was. Everyone he met seemed to want to do something for him.

When his brother Chuck came to visit David, he couldn't believe his brother's lifestyle. "This is awesome," he told David. "You've got it made."

But it just didn't seem satisfying. David couldn't help feeling something was wrong. Yet he didn't understand why.

"Success was sort of like cotton candy. It tastes great when you first put it in your mouth, but it dissolves real quick," David says. "I'd gotten a lot of success very quickly, made a lot of money, had all the nice toys that I wanted, but it didn't make me happy. There was no real substance to it. It was neat, but it just dissolved away to nothing. You wake up in the morning and you still have to look at yourself in the mirror and wonder what kind of man you're going to be."

The truth was, fame and fortune had already begun to change David. Other people still saw him as a great guy and a wonderful role model. But he says, "When I looked at myself, I didn't like the person I was becoming. I felt I was so important. I had a selfishness and an arrogance. If I was thirty minutes late, I'd think, *It doesn't matter, because they can't start without me. I'm the one who counts.* I found myself doing that more and more.

"I was unsettled—happy one day, sad the next. If the press wrote a critical article about me, I'd down. If everyone was patting me on the back I'd feel great." He was taking his cues from everyone else's opinion of him and that was always changing. He knew he needed something else on which to base his feelings—and his life.

During the 1990-91 season, a man by the name of Greg Ball, from an organization called Champions for Christ, approached David one day after a Spurs' practice. He said he was a minister and had been praying especially for him. But as soon as David heard Greg's words, he quickly apologized, "Oh, I gotta go. Maybe we can talk another time."

In June of 1991, David saw Greg Ball again and agreed to give him a few minutes of his time. They went to David's home, and after a little casual conversation, Greg asked, "David, do you love God?"

"Of course I love God," David replied, a little surprised by the question.

"How much time do you spend praying?"

"Every once in a while. Before I eat. Sometimes before I go to bed."

"How much time do you spend reading the Bible?" Greg asked.

"I've got one around here somewhere," David replied, feeling a little uneasy. "I just don't understand very much of it."

Greg Ball pressed on, "When you love someone, don't you usually take time to get to know them?"

"Sure," David agreed. He didn't say it, but he was thinking, *But God isn't a real person.*

"The Old Testament says to set aside one day a week to honor God," Greg was saying. "When was the last time you spent one day, not one day a week, but just one day praising God and thanking him for what you have?"

David finally understood why he'd been feeling so uneasy. He thought, *I've never given God a day to pray and thank him! I really have been acting like a spoiled brat. Everything has been about me, me, me. How much money can I make?*

My life is all about David's praise, David's glory. I play basketball to hear everybody cheering me and have them pat me on the back. I've never stopped to honor God or really think about all he has given me.

David suddenly felt so ashamed he began to cry, and he couldn't stop. He cried all afternoon. He realized God was very real, and that God had sent Greg Ball to deliver this message. All the material things he had really were like cotton candy— nothing to them. They couldn't do anything to fill up his empty soul.

It scared David to realize that, "Without God, I have nothing. I am nothing." He closed his eyes and prayed.

He told God how sorry he was for the ungrateful way he'd been acting and living. "Everything you've given me," he told the Lord, "I'm giving back to you today."

He knew his life had been changed forever that afternoon. But David wasn't sure what to do next. Greg Ball handed him a Bible and told him it was "the manual for life."

David was an engineer—a tinkerer who always wanted to know how things worked. He actually read manuals for fun just to learn how some computer or new software worked. The Bible was a manual? For life? No kidding!

Greg Ball says David was "like a sponge." He got so excited about what he was learning that he called his brother to tell him he was reading the Bible!

"David," Chuck told him, "you're scaring me!"

But the truth of what he was feeling and learning really came home to him a few days later. David watched on television as the Bulls celebrated their first championship. He says, "I saw Michael Jordan hugging that trophy and I remember thinking, *Wow! I've always wanted to be like Mike, right? Win the championship, be the best player in the game. I want all the stuff he has.* But as I watched him kiss that trophy, I thought, *That's great right now. But in six months people will be telling him, 'Magic has five of those. You only have one.'*

"And it hit me again. Pursuing success is like chasing your tail. You can never win. Proving yourself to others is like trying to catch the wind. No matter what you do, someone always raises the bar. Or they start tearing you down. And I realized if that's where I was going, I was in a lot of trouble. That's a road to nowhere. It's like running after a rainbow. The world's idea of success is never going to fulfill me. There really has to be another way."

David was now sure he'd finally found it.

14

A NEW MAN

I was reading the Bible three and four hours a day," David says. "And I couldn't believe how much I was learning. The words just seemed to jump off the page at me. I had no idea all that wisdom was in there. It was like the Lord speaking to me. It was so clear all of a sudden."

David quickly realized his new commitment to God meant he would be a new man. But he never imagined all the ways his new faith would change his life.

Most people who had known David Robinson hadn't seen any reason for him to change. He was one of the finest role models in sports—not just an athlete, but a scholar, a good citizen, an officer, and a gentleman. He always stood ramrod straight throughout the playing of the national anthem. He was so squeaky clean he didn't even drink or smoke. He regularly spoke at school assemblies telling kids to stay in school and off of drugs.

The Admiral was truly admirable. What was there not to like? When people first heard that he'd become a born-again Christian, many people wondered why in the world David thought he needed to change?

"But they only saw me from the world's perspective," David says. "And the world doesn't have very high standards to live up to. We all can compare ourselves to someone we think is worse than we are and decide we're pretty good people. I did that." Plus David had a lot of other people telling him what a good person he was. So he says he had to understand that he didn't come close to measuring up to God's standard. He knew he needed Christ's presence and help in his life.

David says that one of the Bible passages he found most helpful is from the gospel account of Jesus asking, "If a blind man leads a blind man, will they both fall into the pit?" He says it hit him: "I am a blind man. How can I encourage someone else when I don't know where I'm going myself? I was only beginning to see things from God's perspective. I finally had something to give somebody else."

"I remembered all those times I'd gone to high schools to tell kids to Say NO! to drugs. Now I realized I hadn't been giving the kids anything real. Maybe they were impressed with me for a few moments, but I could never change their lives. However, if I could give them Christ, he could change their lives through and through. So it was a great feeling to know that from now on when I shared with people, it wasn't just me anymore. God would work through me. And he could reach and change peoples' hearts."

One of the biggest surprises resulting from David's new faith involved his love life. He'd broken up with a young woman named Valerie Hoggatt a few months earlier. He'd been introduced to her by a friend while on temporary Naval duty in Southern California back in 1988. They dated a number of times, and when he'd returned to Kings Bay (GA) Naval Submarine Base, their relationship continued long distance. She came to see him. He visited her. And Valeria became his steady girlfriend.

But she was his ex-girlfriend by the time he'd committed his life to God. He'd broken up with her. "I told Valerie that she loved me too much," David says. "That I could never have the love for her, the passion for her, that she had for me. And I needed to find someone I could love as much as she loved me."

But now as David read his Bible and prayed for God to give him direction in life, he kept thinking about Valerie. How could he have said what he said to her? It had been another area of his life where he'd been incredibly selfish. She'd been so loving toward him, and he hadn't even really tried to love her the same way.

David called Valerie and told her he'd been reading the Bible and had given his life to God. She told him that she too had been studying the Bible and growing closer to the Lord. "We got back together," David says. "We read the Bible together. She was the same sweet, wonderful person she had been before. I just hadn't been paying attention. Our whole relationship was different now that God was in it."

Three months later, David stunned Valerie when he asked her to marry him. She said yes and they were married in December 1991 at Tired Stone Baptist Church in San Antonio. The national media reported on the wedding from outside the church. Only family, a few friends, and a number of David's teammates witnessed the private ceremony.

Everyone was happy for the new couple. David's coach even speculated that having a wife to go home to might help stabilize the personal life of his star and perhaps even make him a better basketball player. But there were many observers who worried and openly wondered if David's new faith might have an opposite effect.

One criticism heard about David through the years is that he's too nice. He doesn't have a competitive nature—the killer instinct needed to win a championship, "He's too thoughtful, too bright, and he has too many other interests to devote himself totally to basketball," people would say. No one ever questioned his physical skills, but some people did wonder about his commitment to the game. Many of them expected David's new faith to weaken his game by making him "soft." At the very least, they thought it might be yet another interest that would absorb so much of his time and attention that it would take away from his commitment to competitive basketball.

They need not have worried. As outstanding as David had been in his first two years as a professional, he continued to improve. He had another All-NBA season in 1991-92. Unfortunately, he had to have surgery when he tore a ligament in his hand in the spring and thus had to sit and watch his teammates eliminated in the first round of the playoffs. He did recover in time to join the rest of the original Olympic Dream Team and capture the gold medal in the Barcelona Summer Games.

The 1992-93 Spurs went through a lot of turmoil as a team when their new coach resigned suddenly after a disappointing start. The team rallied under yet another coach, John Lucas. David again put in an All-Star season and led an injury-plagued team to the playoffs where they lost again. In 1994, after being seen early in his career primarily as a defensive and rebounding force, David led the NBA in scoring. He captured the season scoring title, beating out Shaquille O'Neal, by racking up an amazing 71 points in his final regular season game.

Asked about the role his faith played in his career, David told *Sports Illustrated* that rather than weakening his game, he believed it had helped make him better. As a Christian, he came to realize that playing basketball was a God-given gift—and it was his duty to make the most of that gift.

"I'm not playing for the fans or the money," he told the magazine, "but to honor God." That was now his motivation. "So every night I get out there and try to honor him and play great."

David also believed that the better he played, the more people would listen to him, and the greater would be his opportunity to influence others for Christ.

His new, higher motivation obviously worked. His coach John Lucas called David "the best basketball player in the game—there has never been another player like him."

The coach of the rival Seattle Supersonics, George Karl, said about the improvement, "This is a different David Robinson than we've seen in the past. He's a much more dangerous player. I've always said the man, if he would ever commit to winning, would be as scary as anybody in the league."

Off the court, no one called him scary. But he may have been even more impressive there. Even before he'd become a Christian, David believed he needed to give back to the community. He not only got involved with the fifth-grade class at Gates Elementary but now as a Christian, he and Valerie contributed 10 percent of their earnings to numerous charities and churches in and around San Antonio. They started and funded The Robinson Foundation to channel their giving, distributing over a million dollars to various causes in the first three or four years and investing another million to be used in future work.

Some of the charities provide jackets and shoes in cold weather. The Robinsons help sponsor Christian camps and after-school programs. They give money to programs encouraging young people to abstain from drugs, alcohol, and premarital sex. David runs a Christmas toy drive every year to brighten the holidays of thousands of children. Number 50 donates 50 tickets to every Spurs home game. Those tickets go to kids who have been nominated by their teachers for outstanding achievement in the classroom.

Anyone who thought his generosity made the perennial All-Star seem too good to be true probably thought the same thing about the way he played in the 1994-95 season. After leading his team to a fantastic 60-22 record in the regular season, the announcement came just before the opening game of the NBA playoff series against Hakeem Olajumon and the Houston Rockets that he'd won the year's Most Valuable Player award.

But neither the season record, the MVP trophy, nor David's strong personal performance made any difference. Hakeem played even better than David did, and Houston won the Western Conference Finals in six games.

David, his teammates, and the San Antonio fans had been so convinced this was the Spurs' year that it seemed impossible to accept the defeat. "It felt like falling off a cliff," David admitted, "to go from something so high to something so low in such a short time. I don't think there's any worse feeling for an athlete than to feel inadequate. These are the times when you really have to love the game, when you realize you were six games away from a title, and now you have to start all over again."

He had to wonder if he and the Spurs would ever enjoy an NBA championship.

15

TRUE SUCCESS

A very successful 1995-96 season also ended for David without the long-sought NBA championship. But that disappointment was eased a bit later in the summer when David and his U.S. teammates won the gold medal during the Atlanta Olympic Games. David became the first and only American male basketball player to enjoy the honor of competing in three Olympics.

The following injury-plagued year proved to be the most difficult and frustrating season in David's career. After winning a franchise-high 62 games in 1994-95 and following that with 59 victories in 1995-96, expectations were again high for the San Antonio team. But this time the dreams were shattered by injuries to several key players.

After missing the beginning of the season with back problems, David returned only to break his foot. He managed to play about half the minutes in just six games. Without him, the Spurs won only twenty games all season and missed the playoffs for the first time since he joined the team.

His injuries caused David to wonder about his chances of ever winning an NBA title. But his limitations on the court didn't stop him from making the most of life off the court.

Not having to travel all season with his team enabled David to spend more time at home with his family. He and Valerie have three young boys—David Jr., Corey, and Justin. David says the experience has taught him that fatherhood is, by far, a tougher and more important job than being a professional basketball player.

"The responsibility is huge," he says. "You realize that you're impacting their lives. You try to set a standard. I really take it very seriously. It's fun. But it's also challenging." And when it comes to basketball versus fatherhood, he says his kids are his higher priority.

Another priority is David's continuing determination to give back to his community. Knowing that he couldn't personally provide scholarships and encouragement for all the needy children in San Antonio like he had for the Gates Elementary students, David came up with a better, long-range strategy. In 1997, he and Valerie announced they were donating $5 million, the largest single monetary gift in history given by a sports star, to help build a Christian school, the Carver Academy. Its mission would be to provide academically outstanding educational opportunities for the children of the city's Eastside.

At least one more good thing resulted from San Antonio's terrible season record that year. The Spurs were given a place in the draft lottery—and they struck gold. After winning the number one pick in the 1997 NBA draft, the Spurs landed super-prospect Tim Duncan, a multi-talented, 7-foot, Wake Forest All-American.

Some observers wondered how David would react to sharing the Spurs' stage with a highly touted newcomer. A lot of veteran stars might have been jealous or sulked, but not the Admiral. Soon after Duncan signed his contract, David invited the rookie to join him at his summer home in Colorado.

For almost two weeks, David and his new teammate ran conditioning drills up and down Aspen Mountain and then practiced together in a local high school gym. Impressed not only with Duncan's talent but also his willingness to work and learn, David let his new friend know he wanted to do everything possible to help him do his best.

Together, the teammates suddenly turned the Spurs fortunes around. Opponents who managed to slow down one of them seldom stopped the other. David concentrated more on defense and distributing the scoring. For the first complete season since he joined the team, he wasn't his team's leading scorer or rebounder. Tim Duncan edged him out in both categories as he won Rookie of the Year honors and drew tremendous acclaim as the greatest impact player to join the league since Shaquille O'Neal.

In the meantime, some observers questioned whether David's reduced stats were an indication that his skills were deteriorating with age. Wiser observers praised him for his selflessness in assisting Tim's success and understanding that the team was stronger than ever because of David's willingness to take a different, more specialized, and perhaps "lesser" role.

David now says he probably got too much credit for accepting a "reduced" role because it seemed to him like a no-brainer. "My skills always lent themselves to being a cleanup man, playing defense, disrupting a game, and making things happen," he says. "Tim's talents make him the perfect go-to guy—he has all the hook shots and other nice moves."

Still, David admits it's not always easy to share the glory. "Sure," he says, "it's great to be 'The Man'—getting all the attention and the accolades when you win. But we're a better team now with the credit and the glory shared.

"I was frustrated for ten years without a championship—always trying to figure out what more I could do. It's been an important life lesson to realize I couldn't do that by myself either."

That long-awaited championship finally did come in 1999, the second season David and Tim were teammates. The Spurs downed the New York Knicks in the finals four games to one.

The buzzer sounded with the usual post-game celebration—everyone running around hugging everyone else. But David says, "I was just dazed. My mind was saying, *Is it over?* One minute you're still climbing, and the next minute everything you've been working for is right there. The suddenness of it can throw you for a loop. Yes, it was a thrill. But after ten years in the NBA, all my emotion wasn't going to come out in one moment.

"I'm sure some of my teammates had a pretty wild party after we won the championship," David says. But he'd promised David Jr. he could sleep next to Dad if the Spurs won game five, and the poor boy had actually cried when San Antonio fell behind in the second half. So how did the Spur's star center celebrate his team's last-minute victory? He hurried back to his New York hotel room, climbed into bed beside his six-year-old son, and went to sleep.

Later as David reflected on his feelings about the championship, he again credited his faith. He said that being a Christian not only helped motivate him but also helped him deal with the ego and pride issues of playing alongside a great player like Tim Duncan.

He admitted, "I can't deny it felt weird to see Tim standing on the podium with the Finals MVP trophy. I was thinking, *Man, never have I come to the end of a tournament and not been the one holding up that trophy.* It was hard. But I thought about the Bible story of David and Goliath. David helped King Saul win the battle, but the king wasn't happy because he had killed thousands of the enemy while David had killed tens of thousands. So King Saul couldn't enjoy the victory. He was too worried about David getting more credit than he was. I'm blessed that God has given me the ability to enjoy the victory. So Tim killed the tens of thousands. That's great. I can be happy for him."

David said he wasn't caught up with the hardware, however. When photographers wanted a picture of him kissing the championship trophy, he refused saying, "I'm not kissing anything that doesn't kiss me back."

He explains, "Everybody thinks the trophy and the ring are the ultimate goals. But as meaningful and valuable as they are, they are just things. They'll wind up on a shelf somewhere." Life would go on.

"The journey, the experience of winning it will be in my heart forever," David says about the momentous event. And David wouldn't mind winning another. He was deeply disappointed when the Spurs were eliminated from the playoffs in the 2000 and 2001 seasons. He helped convince Tim Duncan to sign a new contract in 2000, committing himself to stay in San Antonio. And in 2001, David signed a contract for less than he might have gotten as a free agent in order to stay in San Antonio for the remainder of his professional career.

David did so hoping for another shot at a championship, but more importantly, he wanted to finish out his career in San Antonio where he has learned there are more important things in life than basketball—in a city where he believes God still has more for him to do.

He wants to see the Carver Academy, which opened in the fall of 2001, grow and provide a brighter educational future for the children of San Antonio's Eastside. When the time comes to walk off the court at the end of his career, David's not sure what he'll do.

"I don't see how I can get away from some kind of ministry," he says. "God's made that a part of my life. I know he wants me to share the Gospel somehow. I'm not a preacher. I'm more of a teacher. Education has always been important to me. I would enjoy teaching Bible study. So I expect he'll want me to do something along those lines. Whether it will be inside or outside a church situation, I don't know.

"Right now I know I'm where God wants me to be," he says, "and I couldn't be happier. Two years from now, five years from now, I don't know where it will be. But when the time comes, he'll open doors and pave the way for me. He'll make it clear what he wants me to do. And I'll be happy to do it."

David says he's learned so many lessons that he wants to share with other people. For example, he says, "It's important to talk about forgiveness. We all need it. Everyone makes mistakes. But we also need to understand the dangers of sin. I know it's not popular to talk about sin today. Yet God tells us in the Bible that he wants us as his followers to be righteous. 'Be holy. Even as I am holy.' That's what we're supposed to do if we want to follow Christ. And those are incredibly high standards.

"That's what I try to tell kids. We can't be sucked into what the world is trying to teach us. Through television we see all these marriages that really stink, and you see in real life that so many families are splitting up. But with God's help, you can have the kind of marriage he intended, you can love your spouse.

"People laugh and say 'Everyone cheats on his income tax.' But with God's help, you can live with integrity. It shouldn't matter what everyone else does.

"We as Christians need to take a stand for higher standards. All it takes is one little light, one candle in a pitch-black room, to make all the darkness go away. As a Christian, you can be that light. If you light one match, you can find your way around the room. And you can help those who will follow you find their way as well. Kids, and adults as well, need to realize God will show them the way. And he'll help them follow it."

The Admiral has always been a leader. Many people think that's what makes him a wonderful role model. But what makes him a hero in our view is that he now understands that it's even more important to be a follower—of Jesus.

We want to hear from you. Please send your comments about this book to us in care of the address below. Thank you.

Zonder**kidz**™

Grand Rapids, MI 49530
www.zonderkidz.com